WASHOE COUNTY LIBRARY

3 1235 02872 4503

W9-CQZ-758

Damage Noted
H2O damaged
9-24-13 kb/w
WCLS

Copyright © 2002 by Charlotte Dematons
Originally published by
Lemniscaat b.v. Rotterdam under the title *Tobber*
Printed and bound in Belgium
CIP data is available
First U.S. edition

Worry
Bear

Charlotte Dematons

Front Street Lemniscaat
ASHEVILLE, NORTH CAROLINA

It was early morning and the toy store was closed. All the bears were still asleep—except one…

Laundry Bears woke up first.

"Hey, you!" one said. "Give me your sweater. Hurry up now."

The little bear took off his
sweater but said nothing.
He just shivered.

Polar Bears noticed.
One said, "The kid's cold."

The other said,
"Let's warm him up."

Laundry Bear shouted,
"Hey, you shaggy
marshmallows are
crushing him!
Get out of there."

Honey Bear said,
"I bet you're hungry.
Want some honey?"

The little bear
said nothing.

"Don't you know anything?
He's not cold and he's not hungry,"
rumbled Big Boss Bear.
"He's lonely."

"All right, everybody! Let's go see if we can find his family. And remember—be back before the toy store opens."

All the bears started
searching—except one.

"Hi there. I'm Blabber Bear. Who are you?"

The little bear still said nothing.

"That's okay, I know what's the matter.
You're worried, aren't you?
I used to be worried, too.
I was worried to be up so high on the shelf…

I thought I'd fall off and land on the floor,
and then some children would grab me
and squeeze me and not let go,
and their mother would yell at them,
and they'd start crying

and wipe their faces with me
and hug and kiss me
and take me on vacation in a car to a beach
and play with me in the sand and water
and shake me all over. and then we'd go home
all scrunched up in the back seat,
under a blanket, snuggled together..."

"Have you ever seen a child?"
Blabber Bear asked.
"Yes," said the little bear,
speaking at last.

"You have? Where?"
"There!"

The toy store is open.
Now all the bears are
wide awake—except one.
Worry Bear has gone
to sleep.